How to write a Book

Experiences and Strategies

Dr. Rohit Shankar Mane

Ukiyoto Publishing

All global publishing rights are held by

Ukiyoto Publishing

Published in 2022

Content Copyright © Dr. Rohit Shankar Mane

ISBN 9789364943536

*All rights reserved.
No part of this publication may be reproduced, transmitted, or stored in a retrieval system, in any form by any means, electronic, mechanical, photocopying, recording or otherwise, without the prior permission of the publisher.*

The moral rights of the author have been asserted.

This is a work of fiction. Names, characters, businesses, places, events, locales, and incidents are either the products of the author's imagination or used in a fictitious manner. Any resemblance to actual persons, living or dead, or actual events is purely coincidental.

This book is sold subject to the condition that it shall not by way of trade or otherwise, be lent, resold, hired out or otherwise circulated, without the publisher's prior consent, in any form of binding or cover other than that in which it is published.

Dedication

How does a person say "Thanks a lot" when there are so many people around to say "Thanks a lot"? Many people helped me to enhance my writing skills, starting from the First Professor whose guest lecture I attended and after that many people from my society, college, university, who helped me to etc.

I would like to thank my Mother, Father, Sister, and Brother for supporting and encouraging me.

They make my life complete."

I express my deep appreciation to the entire team of Ukiyoto Publishing. You have made publishing a wonderful experience for me. I am also thankful to my family and friends for their abundance of love and kindness."

Acknowledgments

How does a person say "Thanks a lot" when there are so many people around to say "Thanks a lot"? Many people helped me to enhance my writing skills, starting from the First Professor whose guest lecture I attended and after that many people from my society, college, university, who helped me to etc.

I would like to thank my Mother, Father, Sister, and Brother for supporting and encouraging me.

They make my life complete.

Contents

How I Revealed My Writing Skills	1
How I Manage Time	16
How I Imagine My Story Chracters?	30
How do I Getting Writing Ideas?	42
How I Make Space for Writing	58
How do I develop Characters?	73
How to be the disciplined Writer	86
How do I Improve Vocabulary	95
About the Author	*111*

How I Revealed My Writing Skills

On a rainy spring day in 2014, I shambled into the guest lecture hall at my university to listen to the guest lecture entitled "How to become a writer".
I was deeply, deeply unhappy.
Writing ironically was my bread and butter at that time.
I spent my last three years surrounding subjects, books, papers for understanding writing.

2 How to write a book

To understand the writing process, I helped different academic writers, scientists, teachers but I haven't got anything because I was not able to understand the selection of subjects for the writing process, selection of objectives, selection of tasks, material collection, selection and many more.

I needed a friend to even help me with this.

My thinking process and heart were somewhere locked away in my cupboard at home therefore I was not able to link my feelings with my thinking level for the writing.

I was helpless.

The first 10 pages of my novel which I have been writing for six months.

Only where was the time?

I was then slumped at my desk on that rainy spring day when my friend arrived, was saying that everyone was welcome to attend the guest lecture at the hall.

I saw him with the lecture title and my study timetable.

Restlessly sat on my wooden chair which was my best chair in front of my desk.

I was thinking,

I was Happy,

I was crying,

I was out of this world.

Fully thinking about "how to be a writer"

Suddenly grabbed my notebook, pen, and water bottle.
Started to run towards guest lecture hall.
Finally, reached there.
The notes I made, prepared during that lecture remain stuck to the corkboard, above my desk two years and one novel later.
They contain no insights into how to shape a compelling plot.
There is nothing on writing convincing dialogue or characterization.
There are no well-worn pearls of wisdom on the importance of cutting adverbs, though you should cut your writing adverbs otherwise story won't get an efficient baseline. But writing a novel demand far more than the word we place on the page. So, in this book, I am going to tell my own story that "how I became a Writer"
During writing, I took some discissions and goals in the view of writing a novel by subject and specifications. These all discissions and goals helped me a lot during my writing of an academic book and novel. It was my start so the first thing did that decided specific goal. That was tough for me but my intention was to be a writer one day. I was mesmerized with that lecture and lecture notes so I was starting my writer journey. It did not bother me

that I would put my writing manuscript aside for time being and why should it bother me?

I would get there at last.

The problem when our goals aren't specific is that it's all too easy to convince ourselves that we are getting there when actually, we were not.

When I was at the University, I mate a young writer of our time. This writer was an eighteen-year-old guy and English was not his first language. You would think this young man wouldn't stand a chance at building a thriving novel-writing career, and yet he did in less than one year.

I knew that if he could do it, I could do it, and I would do it. So many times, when I felt like throwing in the towel, I thought about this writer who made it, against all chances.

It can be difficult to truly save the attainment of ill-defined goals because it is not so clear when we have achieved them. it is very easy to attain the wrong goals but not the correct ones because to achieve correct goals, first one has to go through the wrong goals. then and then only one can earn and learn correct goals. And that person will write happily.

I replaced my goals "how to be a Writer" with "I will write something today".

That was pretty specific.

On the first day of positivity, wrote a page.

The next day deleted the same page but also, wrote a paragraph.

Deleted that paragraph too.

I was going through the literature, videos, recordings, books, but at the end of the 10 days, I had written 20 pages that would never make it into my novel or any book but I would also write what would become the first line statement of my novel. but these 20 days helped me to improve my confidence level as a writer to write something. Also, these days taught me that "I can also write something and connect my heart with my feelings".

Slowly my thinking level was building towards writing. I remember, I was considered a good writer in school; I've always had a natural talent for putting words on paper and making them flow well. I've never been the best writer in the school; however, I realize that I didn't need to be to find success. To be a fruitful writer, being a solid advertiser is objective, and I realize that I had that expertise in me.

The second and most important thing is that we have to make sure our goals and their achievability.

I was writing pages daily.

I was deleting pages daily.

My novel was progressed as I knew with high expectations that my central character and story would unfold.

I was writing pages.
Deleting pages.
Trying to build my central character.
Building my story………
Doing additions, deletions.
I was doing all the possible things that would help to build my story.
I was using reference books.
The book I purchased was an overpriced author guide book. The advice was obsolete.
Felt bad.
Took coffee.
And sat on my wooden chair in front of my desk.
Thinking.
I was holding coffee in one hand and dancing pen in another hand.
Thinking.
Suddenly stopped another hand and dancing pen.
Took pen and note book.
I set difficult goals to myself.
That today I will write some positive points of my central character and within 20 days I will finish 5 chapters. Next five days I will review it. Next week, I will send a sample of my novel writing to publisher, I will review comments. I will correct it. I will finalize it.

When I decided to replace my goal "how to be a Writer" with "I will write something today".

Because of that, got confidence, got very clear ideas, very specific with my goals, and felt awesome because this was achievable.

Huuuussshhh….

I took long breath and felt helpless.

I laughed and said "I can write now"

I was able to write something.

I was able to build my central character.

I was able to move my writing pages full of words.

We all too often set goals for ourselves that are unachievable but I would like to say to all that you should set a goal that is achievable. Because goals are nothing but hopes, nothing but happiness, nothing but morality towards our feelings. And sometimes these unachievable goals give us unhappiness and we feel very bad about ourselves for getting failure. Then we feel to not to try. These feelings would make our death in a live body.

Many writers set different goals for themselves such as subject area, chapter number, word count, page number, publisher, and many more. This will help you to think in restricted areas and levels. This is also the best option for writing a novel but it always won't work for all.

I also used this trick.

I thought to write 10 pages per day and that was not so much, but still, I struggled with it.

I got scared.

It made me cry in front of my goals.

I stopped and decided to set myself an achievable goal that I can do.

If a goal is not in my area or I am not achieving the goal after trying also. Many more tries.

So, I told myself that

"Rohit, do you know? Such goals are not achievable for me.

I told myself to spend time with my central character, with my story, with my other side characters the story, my laptop, my feelings, and my heart. It doesn't really matter that "I have written 100 words a day and deleted 200 words in one hour"

No right?

What matters is to build my novel story and characters.

Time is most important.

we always say that for a good relationship, time is important like this for a good novel Storytime is important. we have to spend time with our loved ones and write also.

But during writing, we have to be focused, clear, hard with time, bound with characters, story, and material.

"You will feel alone and die-off"

You should be strong, and clear with all ideas.
I submitted my sample chapter to the publisher and after 1 week I got mail that your sample chapter got rejected.
Felt bad.
Felt helpless.
Not able to concentrate on writing.
Took the day off, a week off, and 10 days off.
Stopped writing.
Stopped thinking.
Denied to seat on my wooden chair in front of my desk.
Deleted my story characters from my feelings and heart.
Closed them in the cupboard at my home.
Felt meaningless.
Here I learned, how to accept rejections.
"Be prepared for failure"
You will fail. It's inescapable, so you should start getting ready for it now. The disappointment might be little, similar to, say, committing an error on a client commitment. Or then again it could be very terrific, such as losing an employment you esteemed. How you handle that disappointment can raise or lower the dangers of bombing once more - and shape your heritage as a pioneer.

Certain individuals handle these difficulties well. Others not really well. In my work, I've noticed a few normal topics among those pioneers who will generally adapt especially successfully to the unpreventable.

Recognize the disappointment and put it in context.

You can't start to return quickly from a slip-up in the event that you don't concede you've made it. As clear as it sounds, it's obviously not generally simple to do.

Research shows that taking ownership of their slip-ups is the key element isolating the individuals who handle disappointment well from the people who don't. The individuals who were wrecked perseverated and didn't converse with others about it. They made little endeavor to correct the results. The people who weren't wrecked did the inverse: They conceded their mix-ups, acknowledged liability, and afterward took more time to fix the issue. Also, a while later, they continued to forget about it and continue on. Search for purposes, not fault. Assuming you've caused an issue, fortunately you have command over that reason.

By zeroing in on finding the cause(s), as opposed to relegating fault (with all the worth decisions that go with that), you assume command and move to keep comparative disappointments from reoccurring. Thinking as far as causes instead of fault is like embracing what Carol Dweck portrays as a "development situated" as opposed to a "fixed" attitude.

A proper attitude will in general pass on us vulnerable and prepared to shrink even with a test. A development attitude sets us in a situation to go ahead toward progress. Before you wrack your mind to concoct a proper reaction, have some time off.

Move away from the job that needs to be done for some time and allowed your cerebrum to pull together. Not even one of us is intended to work all day, every day, except directly following disappointment, it's frequently difficult to quit pondering what's occurred.

As outlandish as it sounds, this is likely the last thing you ought to do. Participate in different pursuits. Invest energy with friends and family, read, or absolutely get some rest. Active work is an or more (we are in general acquainted with the impacts of endorphins on mind movement). It doesn't make any difference what amount of time of a break you require: five minutes, five hours, five days.

The point is to allow your brain to meander. You'll be flabbergasted at what you concoct.

As I referenced above, disappointment, similar to death and expenses, is unavoidable. In any case, the thing about disappointment that is the greatest wellspring of uneasiness is you frequently don't have the foggiest idea when or where it will strike. You could be working at something for quite a long time just to have it breakdown in a day, and that is alarming. Thusly, I advocate getting ready for disappointment. Some might blame me for being excessively negative, and I get that. Just from the phrasing, "planning for disappointment" seems like "anticipating the most awful," however that truly isn't the thing I'm getting at.

Getting ready for disappointment basically implies finding some peace with disappointment being an inescapable piece of life.

Considering inability to be inescapable, and not as some fear phantom coming to torment you, is more sensible, and will help you not respond so disastrously when you truly do definitely come up short at something.

The important thing is to see the failure in your journey with struggle then will you can understand and celebrate the success.

All will face failure in their career. Specially writer too much. They will get many rejection letters from different publishers for their work.

"I got sixty rejection letters from sixty publishers"

It means that your writing is not good writing by chance. Your story characters are not built up well.

But that is not you right? Its you're writing.
One day I was not doing anything about my writing but now I trying, I am getting failure letters.
Ok. Not this subject novel but I can write another subject novel, right?
Started another novel writing.
Completed.
Sent to publisher.
Got mail as "its good writing, well established characters, we can publish your novel"
Got happy.
Danced full night.
Drunk my favorite wine.
Danced.
Drunk my favorite wine.
Danced.
Slept happily.
I was encouraged by that letter. It is important to give us ourselves self-motivational talk from time to time. A few words of motivational.
To accomplish significance, you want to quit requesting authorization. For this reason, inspiration is significant in life since it quits clarifying some pressing issues and adjusts you to pursue your objectives.
Objectives are the venturing stones toward your fantasies thus, to accomplish them, you want the

inspiration to keep you moving ahead towards them. Not every person is brought into the world with inspiration.

There is an extreme need some who accept 'I'll get to that one day' or 'there's something wrong with the circumstance' or an exemplary instance of 'I can't do that'. Inspiration is the characterizing factor that transforms a decent thought into prompt activity. It transforms a smart thought into a business and can emphatically affect your general surroundings.

Without inspiration, you can't accomplish anything. There are no goal lines to go for the gold reason to endeavor towards.

Inspiration is a significant fundamental ability. The explanation it's significant is on the grounds that each individual on this planet is interesting and has a reason. To steward your motivation well, you must be roused to pursue your objectives which assists your fantasies with turning into a reality. Not1 only for the good of you, yet the purpose of others also.

You experience a daily reality such that inspiration has tackled issues and delivered items and administrations you never realized you wanted.

Inspiration can likewise help you actually to be the best you can be. This can decidedly affect your certainty, connections and the local area you live in.

In the event that you're as yet not persuaded about developing your inspiration, the following are eight justifications for why inspiration is significant throughout everyday life.

We have to accept facts in daily life. If you tell yourselves that you are the worlds best storyteller then you can run long with your stories. It will increase your confidence. It will increase your words, it will increase your vocabulary, it will increase your characters, it will build up your story and will build up your thinking level with heart.

My first Novel Published entitled "Mine"

That day was 20th March 2017.

It took me three years to became a writer.

How I Manage Time

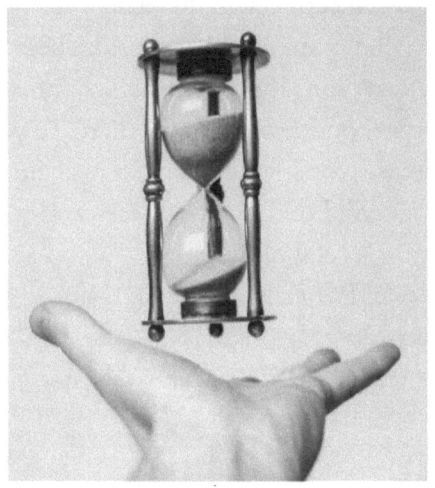

Time management is a very difficult task. When I started my writing career that time the first think came in my mind was time management.

How can I manage time for writing before and after my office work?

Should I wake up early?

Should I sleep late night?

Should I quit job?

should I stay alone?

should I go somewhere in hill station for months?

ohm my god...

my brain was running with different questions and complex directions.

I was not getting what to do?

I woke up.

Bathed with cold water.

Took hot coffee.

went on walk.

Came back to room after two hours and sat on my wooden chair Infront of my desk.

First prepared some questions for my daily schedules on one paper.

Answered for all question one by one.

I wrote all answers on the same paper.

I read it.

I felt to manage my work not time.

so that day I decided something.

I started to manage my work not time.

I was happy.

It's hard to take use of every single minute of our day especially when there are too many daily chores around. Since childhood, our parents and teachers have instructed us to spend time and money sensibly. Using time effectively is the act of dispensing your opportunity to assignments gainfully and productively. Regularly, using time productively includes arranging out your everyday exercises and practicing cognizant control of your experience as you complete those exercises. A few normal topics for viable using time productively incorporate clear objectives, needs, and assumptions.

You can apply the act of using time productively to any piece of your life, including proficient and individual time. Be that as it may, in proficient circles, consummating using time productively is quite possibly the most indispensable abilities worker ought to create.

The first question what I written was, I am wasting how much time?

When I saw and calculated my waste of time.

I got scared.

I told myself that "Rohit You are wasting so much time, stop it".

Many of us are prey to timewasters that steal time we could be using much more productively.

What are your time bandits?

Do you spend too much time Internet surfing, reading email, social media posting, texting, or making personal calls?

I did my own survey of time-wasting.

I was wasting a total of 3 hours a day on different useless work. That I realized.

One hour with internet surfing, using social media, posting on social media, useless calls, etc.

Half an hour with useless calls on useless topics.

A half hour on useless meetings.

One hour with unorganized my work schedule and other things.

I realized.

I deleted these time wasted minutes and work from my list.

I started to track my daily activities which helped to form an accurate picture of how much time I spent on various activities, which is the first step to effective time management.

I asked a second question myself, your aim or goal is fixed?

Have you enlisted all daily goals?

The answer was No.

Keep in mind, that the focal point of using time effectively is really changing your ways of behaving, not evolving time. A decent spot to begin is by taking out your own time-squanderers. For multi-week, for instance, put forth an objective that you won't accept individual calls or answer non-business-related instant messages while you're working.

Consider this an augmentation of the third time usage tip. The goal is to change your ways of behaving after some time to accomplish anything that overall objective you've set for yourself, like expanding your usefulness or diminishing your pressure. So, you want to layout your objectives as well as track them over the long haul to see if you're achieving them.

"Using time effectively can be characterized as bunches of conduct abilities that are significant in the association of study and course load".

Happy time usage abilities have been recognized as having a "buffering" impact on pressure and are a vital sign of better execution and lower pressure and nervousness in advanced education. In any case, numerous writers find it difficult to direct both their investigations and their outer lives.

The Time Management Behavior Scale was created by Macan, Shahani, Dipboye, and Phillips (1990). It recognized and depicted factors inside using time effectively, for example, laying out targets, focusing on assignments, putting forth. Claessen and partners in their review have inferred that variables like the prioritization of undertakings and exercises, appointments, appropriate administration of gatherings, and getting ready for word-related and individual issues are powerful factors impacting using time productively. Therefore, time management is important for writing a novel.

Following are some important time management examples.

- Planning.
- To-do lists and checklists.
- Prioritizing.
- Evaluating urgent tasks.
- Goal setting.
- Auditing and improving workflows.
- Filtering notifications.
- Setting thoughtful deadlines
- Delegation
- Record keeping
- Staff scheduling
- Documentation and project management

- Setting short-and long-term goals
- Stress management
- Using data
- Automation
- Consolidating your technology.

Now the question arises that how you are going to manage all goals or plans for a day.

So, I would like to suggest something for you all people.

You people can use notes books, software, or mobile phones to set your daily goals or aims or daily chores.

These gazettes will help to keep reminders for everything because physically managing your time is to knowing where it's going now and planning how you're going to spend your time in the future.

And how you can do it?

The simple answer is goal prioritization.

Here we must discuss goal prioritization.

Goal prioritization is the method involved with recognizing your targets and sorting out them in view of their direness, worth, and significance. This cycle additionally expects you to fittingly designate your assets, time, and exertion where they're required the most. It's fundamentally an extravagant term for what you could as of now be doing. Determining what to zero in on first prior to continuing to different undertakings.

But at the same time goal prioritization is very important as far as time management is considered.

Goal prioritization is tied in with beginning your day with what makes the biggest difference while yet getting past everything on your plate.

Consider it.

Wouldn't you need to invest the most energy into the objectives that could create the best profit from speculation?

Sure, you do.

And objective prioritization can assist you with distinguishing these goals and planning how to finish them.

It improves goal prioritization regularly prompts less pressure and better usefulness. It can likewise further develop your time usage abilities since it assists you with splitting your time between your objectives.

Are confused with goal prioritization /

Let's consider some theories.

I will make it clear.

Suppose you've proactively defined your objectives and decided all that you'll have to finish them. Every one of the parts is set up, so isn't positioning your objectives simply an additional stage?

Not in the slightest degree!

Regardless, objective prioritization is a critical piece of the usefulness puzzle. The following are a couple of steps that consistently incorporate objective prioritization into what's going on as of now. Thusly, distinguishing significant errands and laying out everyday boundaries can occupy scarcely any time on your timetable.

- Recognize a couple of objectives or goals.
- Separate every objective.
- Measure your advancement.
- Keep yourself responsible.
- Remove interruptions.

For clearer picture let us understand the example.

Envision a glass of pop. Envision presenting yourself with a glass of pop. As the fluid fills the glass, small air pockets ascend to the top. In this model, all the soft drink in the glass addresses your objectives. The air pockets at the top are your needs. Bubble prioritization begins with making a rundown of objectives. Then, you'll look at the main objective of your rundown to the subsequent one and conclude which one is more fundamentally important.

From that point, you'll continue to the third objective and contrast it with the one you recently focused on. When you work your direction down the rundown, the objective you're left with toward the end turns into your first concern. You can then recurrent the cycle with the other objectives, barring the one not set in stone as your need. This strategy can be helpful assuming every one of your objectives appears to be similarly significant and you're having trouble sorting out where to begin. With this strategy, you're contrasting the objectives with one another as opposed to attempting to rank them from a hierarchical view.

Once you prioritize your goals or objectives. You must lay out routines and stick to them however much as could be expected.

How can we prepare layout routines and stick to them however much as could be expected?

Let's see a clearer picture.

Conclude what should be in your daily schedule.

Would you like to get more activity or more alone time?

Focusing on what is critical to you prior to beginning is vital!

Put forth little objectives.

Break every huge objective into more modest objectives. While a major objective is energizing to handle, it regularly prompts disappointment as we take on something over the top. Assuming your general objective is to eat better suppers, begin by transforming one thing daily, consistently, to assemble certainty. At the point when you achieve that, compliment yourself!

Format an arrangement.

Begin with each week in turn and begin little - that way you can expand on straightforward achievements. Compose everything out on a schedule, practically like an arrangement.

Be reliable with time.

If you have any desire to get a day-to-day stroll in, endeavor it simultaneously consistently. Getting done with your responsibilities first thing prior to losing inspiration permits you to appreciate help day in and day out. If you have any desire to get to the rec center, do it as you would prefer to or from work, you will have more achievement. A great many people won't have any desire to take off from the warm house once they return home.

Be ready.

While choosing another everyday practice, ensure you have every one of the pieces before you start; this will make it simpler to begin immediately. For instance, on the off chance that another goal is to clean the house each Saturday morning, ensure your vacuum cleaner is working appropriately and you have all the cleaning materials required.

Make it fun.

Getting into another daily schedule and new objectives aren't generally fun, however, there are ways of making it fun. Track down an exercise amigo, get a decent playlist for cleaning, and attempt new cooking classes - anything to assist you with partaking in your new daily schedule.

Keep tabs on your development.

Make a visual schedule that you can check off every day that you complete the assignment. A great many people would rather not "break the chain" and see a missing spot on their schedule.

Reward yourself.

Whenever you have fallen into daily practice on a predictable premise, reward yourself with something fun. For instance, assuming your objective was to get into everyday practice of getting mess consistently before bed, reward yourself with new shoes that you can appreciate around the perfect house. While emergencies will emerge, you'll be considerably more useful on the off chance that you can follow schedules often. For the vast majority, making and following a normal allows them to get directly down to the undertakings of the day as opposed to squandering time and getting everything rolling.

The start setting time limits for goals or tasks.

For example, perusing and noting email can consume your entire day assuming you let it. All things considered, put down a boundary of one hour daily for this errand and stick to it. (The simplest method for helping square of time to this task instead of noting email on request.)

And try not to waste time waiting for anyone.

From client gatherings to dental specialist arrangements, abstaining from hanging tight for a person or thing's unimaginable. Yet, you don't have to simply stay there and waste time. Innovation makes it simple to work any place you are your tablet or cell phone will assist you with remaining associated. You can be perusing a report, looking at a bookkeeping sheet, or arranging your next showcasing effort.

These all tricks will help everyone with time management and health life.

Compelling time usage abilities don't simply help your expert life yet can likewise work on your life outside of the workplace. Assuming you monitor things on the expert front, you get more opportunities to zero in on your own life and connections. Knowing the way that undertakings and exercises are on target will get a feeling of serenity in your own life. As you feel more settled and less worried, your personal satisfaction improves consequently.

Being dependable with your work won't just build your viability yet will likewise assist you with procuring a decent standing at work. Whenever chiefs and seniors realize that you generally complete your undertakings on schedule, it could lead the way for a more limited time open doors at work.

I also used, used, and will use all these tricks in my daily life so I made my writing very easy and independent of my office work schedule.

You can also use these all tricks and manage time for writing your novel.

How I Imagine My Story Chracters?

Jean Genet says,

"My Books are not novels because none of my characters make decisions on their own"

Characters are the key points of the story. A Character is any individual, creature, or figure addressed in artistic work. Characters are fundamental for a decent story, and the primary characters significantly affect the plot or are the most impacted by the occasions of the story.

Character advancement refers to how created and complex a person is. A few characters begin as exceptionally created. For instance, assuming we know something about how a person strolls and talks, her thought process, who she connects with, and what sort of mysteries she has, she is normally more complicated and created.

Different characters create throughout the span of a story, beginning one way and winding up various, becoming changed by what befalls them. Or on the other hand you could see one side of the person for some time yet sooner or later, another side is uncovered, demonstrating the person to be more mind boggling.

The universally useful of characters is to broaden the plot. Numerous accounts utilize various kinds of characters. Each story should have principle characters. These are the characters that will meaningfully affect the plot or are the most impacted by what occurs in the story. There are numerous ways of classifying principle characters: hero or adversary, dynamic or static person, and round or level characters. A person can likewise regularly squeeze into more than one class or travel through classifications.

Practically every story has somewhere around one hero. A hero is a primary person who produces the activity of a story and draws to the peruser's advantage and compassion. The hero is frequently the legend or courageous woman. For instance, in the well-known Divergent set of three, the hero is Tris. The story is told according to her perspective, and she is vital to all the activity in the plot. The hero is generally a very much evolved character; along these lines, she is more engaging.

Something contrary to the hero is the main enemy. A main enemy is a person who goes against the hero. In that equivalent book series, Tris is gone against both by Eric, a perverted mentor, and Jeanine Matthews, a coldblooded, biased researcher. Together, the hero or heroes and bad guy or enemies move the plot along, make the activity, and draw the peruser's advantage.

The idea of dynamic and static characters is intently attached to character advancement. A powerful person is one who goes through some kind of progress; they show character advancement. A hero is typically a powerful person. In the Divergent series, Tris is a unique person since she transforms from a timid, frail young lady into a solid, certain lady.

Tobias, who later turns into Tris' beau, is likewise a unique person. He transforms from a hard, cold, and far off individual to somebody who has shortcomings, shows extraordinary love, and winds up battling for the long term win close by Tris.

Static characters, then again, are the individuals who don't adjust all through the direction of the story. They effectively show differentiation to dynamic ones, declining to develop and staying in one spot or mindset. In Divergent, the two enemies, Eric and Jeannine, stay mean and savage all through the series.

The idea of round and level characters is additionally intently attached to character improvement. Round characters are completely evolved figures in the story. They are more practical and complex and show a genuine profundity of character. They require additional consideration from the peruser; they can settle on astounding choices or bewildering ones. Many variables can influence round characters, and they respond to those factors everything being equal. In Divergent, Tobias substantiates himself to be a round character. As his past maltreatment by his dad and his shunning and forlornness from being dissimilar are uncovered, we start to see a lot further side to him.

A frog, a bird, a canine, a sheep, a pig, a crow. That sounds like the eating routine for something that eats a wide range of creatures, yet it's simply a rundown of certain characters we can find in stories we read. Whenever we read a story, it is vital we recognize who is essential for it and their job. We need to move toward character examination through three fundamental stages. Try not to skip or change the request for any means since that will remove your capacity to examine the text appropriately.

These are the three stages:

Appreciate: Gain an essential comprehension subsequent to perusing the story

Decipher: Dig further into the subtleties

Make inferences: Using what was gained from stages one and two, you can reach scientific determinations

We should find out about the three little pigs and the large terrible wolf and afterward examine the characters.

Quite a long time ago, there were three little pigs who lived with their grandma. As they became older, the most youthful but most adult, concluded they ought to all form houses for themselves. The other two siblings concluded that would be smart. The most seasoned, who could have done without to work and was languid, constructed a place of feed. The center sibling, who needed to play the entire day constructed a place of wood. The most youthful, and savvies, fabricated a place of block.

At some point, the large terrible wolf emerged from the woodland and thumped on the entryway of the place of feed. Then he blew the house down. The pig got away and raced to the place of wood. Then, the wolf blew down the place of wood. The two pigs got away and rushed to the place of block. The wolf, expecting the third house was just about as feeble as the other two, endlessly blew with no benefit. He then, at that point, attempted the stack. The most astute pig assembled a fire at the lower part of the smokestack and consumed the wolf, who then took off and stayed away forever.

Always ask questions to yourselves about characters such as

- Who are the characters?
- Who is the protagonist?
- Who is the antagonist?

In The Three Little Pigs, there are three pigs, a grandma pig and a wolf. The most youthful pig is the hero, and the wolf is the main enemy. The hero is the primary person that addresses the legend, and the main bad guy is the one that goes against the hero (the trouble maker).

To decipher the characters, we need to dig somewhat more profound into the subtleties than in the understanding stage. We can pose inquiries about their characteristics, conduct, discernment and reason.

Character qualities pose inquiries like:

- What would we be able to talk about the person's character?
- What does the person resemble, and how would they dress?
- Where are the characters from?
- What is their societal position and monetary foundation?

The most youthful pig is astute, patient and mature. The center pig is perky. The most seasoned pig is sluggish and avoids difficult work. The wolf is depicted as large and terrible. He appears to be ravenous and persevering with a sound arrangement of lungs.

Character conduct pose inquiries like:

- How does the person answer impediments?
- How does the person communicate with different characters?

- For what reason does the person act that way?

The most youthful pig, when confronted with an impediment, thinks about a decent arrangement and makes a move. He assembles a solid block house and furthermore fabricates a fire in the smokestack to hinder the wolf since he is the astute pig. The center pig takes the simple way while building a house and takes off from his concern (the wolf) since he isn't cantered to the point of doing things admirably. The most established pig likewise takes the simple way while building a house and takes off from his concern (the wolf) since he is excessively sluggish. The wolf utilizes his solid power while confronting snags since he is huge and awful.

Character insights pose inquiries like:

- How does the person see oneself?
- What do different characters say about the person in question?
- What does the creator or storyteller say about the person?

In novels different characters are always revealed with different visuals. One of the characters is static character.

A static character is a person that doesn't change in a significant manner throughout the span of the story.

Gain proficiency with the meaning of a static person, investigate how they are not the same as powerful characters, find their motivation, and survey instances of them in mainstream society. Each story needs convincing characters. The characters give it life. They make the world the creator makes genuine to the crowd. These characters should acceptable and persuade. The crowd is an incredible appointed authority at what is reliable with a person's character and what isn't. Incredible creators can make striking characters with unmistakable characters. Both dynamic and static characters can have exceptional characters, however the profundity of their characters lays out the distinctions between these two kinds of characters.

There are two principle kinds of characters. The main sort is the unique person. Creators of grasping stories can give beautiful characters that can create and develop all through the story. These are the powerful characters. Dynamic characters change somehow or another.

The subsequent primary sort of character is the static person. Static characters are something contrary to dynamic; static characters don't change. The character of that character when he is presented is similar character when the story comes to a nearby. And every one of his activities in the middle of stay consistent with that character.

In The Lion King model, Scar would be a static person. He is shrewd and self-serving at the outset, and he keeps those qualities until he kicks the bucket.

One more incredible illustration of a static person is the title character in 'Tear Van Winkle.' When the peruser meets Rip, he is a laid-back, inactive man who disregards his family tasks. Following a 20-year rest, during which Rip's old neighbourhood definitely changes, his character continues as before.

He observes his little girl, presently grown up, and gets back to his inactive and lazy life. Tear is a static person.

In novels different characters are always revealed with different visuals. One of the characters is dynamic character.

A dynamic character is a person who shifts all through the direction of a story because of the struggles they experience on their excursion. A few unique characters get familiar with an illustration, as Harry Potter did in Harry Potter and the Chamber of Secrets. A come to another philosophical comprehension of the world, like Hamlet in the play Hamlet. Others gain development, similar to Prince

Hal in the play Henry IV. Some find blemishes in their perspective, like Sherlock Holmes in 'A Scandal in Bohemia.' Still others find parts of their own character that they didn't know were there, as Neville Longbottom in Harry Potter and the Sorcerer's Stone. These progressions that make a person dynamic are frequently suggested as opposed to expressed altogether, so cautious examination is expected to find them.

For Instance, Harry Potter in Harry Potter and the Chamber of Secrets

One of the principle clashes in Harry Potter and the Chamber of Secrets is Harry's internal struggle. He sees that he imparts a few capacities in like manner to Tom Riddle - who ends up being the underhanded Lord Voldemort - and stresses that this implies he could end up being shrewd also. Dumbledore brings up that Harry is in Gryffindor House, while Tom Riddle was in Slytherin House.

'It (The Sorting Hat) just put me in Gryffindor,' expressed Harry in a crushed voice, since I asked not to go in Slytherin.' 'Precisely,' said Dumbledore, radiating again. 'Which makes you altogether different from Tom Riddle. It is our decisions, Harry, that show the very thing we genuinely are, undeniably more than our capacities.'

This illustration about the significance of one's decisions settle Harry's internal clash and makes him a unique person.

How do I Getting Writing Ideas?

Stories are really fascinating when the principle character needs something strongly. Perusers will continue to peruse to see whether the person accomplishes their objective. The following are a few thoughts for books or stories in light of characters who have strong longings.

- a peruser of romance books who needs to carry on with her very own romantic tale.

- a beginner naturalist whose fantasy is to find another sort of creature.
- a person who needs to accomplish a world record - - he could do without what.
- a person who fantasies about beginning another life in an unfamiliar country.
- a person who needs to burglarize a gem retailer and has an idiot proof (s/he trusts) plan to pull off it.
- a person with no living grandparents, who needs to embrace a grandma.

Here is a list of interesting professions for your main character. See what story ideas they bring to mind.

- Inventor
- Taxi driver
- Magician
- Scuba instructor
- Marriage counsellor
- Prison guard
- Beauty pageant contestant
- Cookbook author
- Computer hacker
- Archaeologist
- Lead singer of an unsuccessful rock band
- Astronaut

- Gossip magazine journalist
- Divorce lawyer
- Animal trainer
- Video game designer
- High school football coach
- Exorcist
- Flight attendant
- Stunt actor

What sort of individual could you hope to find in this calling? Check whether you can play against generalizations and shock the peruser.

What sort of intriguing circumstance could somebody in this calling experience? What difficult situation could he/she run into? How should s/he respond?

Here are some setting thoughts that you can use as story starters. Write a story that takes place.

- in a tattoo parlour
- at the zoo at night
- in an abandoned mental hospital
- in a submarine
- in a magnet factory
- in the vault of a bank
- in a bridal shop
- in the kitchen of Buckingham Palace
- on the edge of a cliff

- entirely in the dark

Adjust a story from reality. You can get convincing plot thoughts by perusing the news or authentic texts or watching narratives. You can likewise utilize a current true to life book to move a made-up novel, brief tale, or content. Thinking all the more comprehensively, you can source motivation from a digital recording, a sonnet, or even a self-improvement guide.

Adjust the plot of a fantasy or people legend. A considerable lot of the best book thoughts come from narrating that rises above different ages.

The realistic novel Sumo by Thien Pham draws on hundreds of years of Japanese practice. The screenplay for The Little Mermaid depended on a Hans Christian Andersen fantasy. Assuming that an incredible story has gotten through the whole way to the current period, there's a decent opportunity its subjects will resound with the present crowds similarly as with past ages.

Make a person in view of somebody you know. Joel and Ethan Coen have said that they concocted the story thought for The Big Lebowski by making a hardboiled analyst thrill ride that highlighted their genuine stoner companion as the criminal investigator. For sure, many writers have mined the characteristics of a dearest companion, relative, or associate as a component of an extraordinary book thought. So whenever you're around individuals you know well, write down a couple of perceptions about their way of behaving either intellectually, in a note pad, or on your telephone and check whether it prompts any story thoughts. Your companion could turn out to be a critical supporting person, or even the primary person.

Expound on a second in your own life. Many writers start their creative cycle by ruminating on an occasion that occurred in their own lives. William Styron drew from his own account as a youthful proof-reader living in Brooklyn when he composed Sophie's Choice.

Judy Blume composed Forever to some degree as an impression of her life as a 17-year-old secondary school understudy.

Examine the plot of a book you appreciate. Return to one of your #1 books, whether that is a new champion or the main book you really cherished as a grown-up. As you reconnect with the plot, contemplate what makes the narrating work for you. Does the book have an unexpected development on each page? Is it a consistently unfurling character study? What components could move plot thoughts for your own story?

Ask yourself "Consider the possibility that?

Think about a known period from history, and envision assuming a couple of key subtleties were changed. This fiction composing strategy is the foundation of a kind known as substitute history fiction. Substitute history fiction is a style of fictitious account where the creator transforms one vital component or components about laid out history and afterward comes up with a story that outcomes from this change.

Embrace the strange.

The absolute best book thoughts might have appeared to be odd from the get go, however they proceeded to create hits that beat hit records. Creators like Kurt Vonnegut, Douglas Adams, John Kennedy Toole, and William S. Burroughs are among the most commended creators of the 20th century, yet large numbers of their clever thoughts could have been shot somewhere around a gamble unwilling distributer. With regards to your own work, don't rush to blue pencil yourself. While not all composing thoughts will yield full-fledged books, it's critical to follow motivation and see where imaginative storylines take you in your book composing venture.

Recollect that numerous a top-of-the-line book was once excused as "excessively revolutionary."

Pick a world in which you need to invest a great deal of energy. Your clever will require your perusers to inundate themselves in a particular world for the hours that they spend perusing. All the more critically, it will require you, the creator, to drench yourself for weeks, months, and even years. Conceptualize a setting and a time-frame that intrigues you and keeps you locked in. Have more than one setting? That is alright, as well, yet don't misjudge the worth of effortlessness with regards to narrating, and don't overstuff your novel with area changes.

Observe a story thought that can support your advantage. Books are something other than a progression of settings and time spans. They should be driven by a story that stays convincing all through its start, center, and end. So, conclude everything story you need to say and be certain it can support an entire book. It doesn't make any difference in the event that you're arranging a legendary dream novel or a picayune dramedy set in an unassuming community. In the event that you figure it may not hold a peruser's advantage for quite a long-time page, consider adjusting your work into a brief tale all things being equal.

Collect a cast of characters. Since you have a world and a story, sort out who the critical figures in this story are. Your fundamental person is clearly the most significant among these. A solid primary person will have a rich and itemized life-from individual history to character characteristics to objectives and aspirations. The more you comprehend your characters, the more you should say about them to a crowd of people.

Plan your completion. Regardless of whether you haven't arranged the start or center of your novel yet, think ahead to a peruser's insight. They will contribute a ton of time perusing your creation, but the piece of your clever that will wait with them most will probably be the consummation. Ensure you're giving them an awesome one, whether you're attempting to compose a smash hit spine chiller or an agonizing, character-driven work of artistic fiction. From your outlook as an author, having a reasonable consummation set up may assist you with building a story that drives toward that closure.

Break the story into acts. Since it has become so obvious where your story is going, now is the ideal time to figure out your account by breaking it into acts. Exemplary stories follow a three-act structure, with each act finishing on a critical second in the general plot. Assuming you pace your account to grow continuously all through the novel, you'll wind up with a book that is reliably great from start to finish.

Begin composing before you experience some sudden nerves. Arranging is fundamental, yet don't allow excessively careful wanting to keep you from the job that needs to be done, which is really composing your book. The principal draft of your first part might be horrible, and it might turn out to be absolutely revamped whenever you're done, yet it's critical to make a plunge before you're deadened by re-thinking.

A person accepts she has carried out a wrongdoing another person realizes she is blameless of.

A hairdresser hears something she shouldn't while trimming hair.

A person awakens knowing another dialect, yet fails to remember their first language.

A mariner ousted to a drawn-out excursion to make up for his violations should accommodate with what he's finished.

A person purchases another coat, just to observe a strange message sewn into its covering.

A person nods off on a neglected boat and rises and shines on another planet.

A family tradition takes steps to self-destruct when an ill-conceived youngster ventures into the image with a rundown of requests.

A person is sold the "Greatest Year of Their Life" by a renowned organization, with the proviso that they should bite the dust a short time later.

A historical center safety officer observers somebody taking a work of art, yet lies about it.

Two towns contend to have the best innovation in the country.

An old lady falls frantically infatuated with a youngster and tempts him.

A took on youngster begins to get many letters from individuals who guarantee they're her folks.

A person's twin kin kick the bucket, and the twin endeavors to fill their shoes.

An overview city endeavors to revive the region by presenting a government.

An alienated family gets together following decade after their grandparents disappear.

A mermaid baits a person into a daily existence undersea.

A working-class family attempts to begin the primary intergalactic news organization involving all the cash in their investment funds.

Amidst a conflict, the ladies of a nearby town leave their area just seven days before their spouses and children return.

A legal advisor surrenders their training to get the nation over with somebody a large portion of their age.

A con artist begins a diary to monitor their double dealing.

A lady chooses to find and gather every one of the dresses her grandma planned.

A parent takes their youngster's development thought and creates a deep-rooted gain they put into retirement.

A person gets back to their old neighbourhood and acknowledges they can at no point leave in the future.

A PC compromises the security of a significant city.

A homicide makes a town betray each other.

A despot powers a famous style fashioner to plan the new military garbs for the conflict.

A loner's guardian dies, constraining her to make trips outside to meet with another possibility for the gig.

An anecdote about an old society where orientation jobs are turned around.

A granddaughter endeavors to associate with her tragically missing grandma by cooking through the family cookbook.

Two separate families become one after a marriage joins them.

A person embarks to cruise the stream from one finish of their country to other.

A person turns into the city chairman of another town that doesn't acknowledge them.

A person finds they can visit the past and future, however at the gamble that they'll lose something important.

A Queen should set up her child to be an appropriate ruler in his late dad's stead.

During the railroad blast, a gathering of homesteaders attempts to stay aware of an evolving society.

A man moves to a provincial town to move away from his inconveniences however inconvenience continues to track down him.

An English extremely rich person chooses to have a progression of challenges to pick a commendable replacement.

On board a separated vessel in Alaska, a group should endure what is happening.

In a progression of week-by-week meetings, a man reviews his experience of Vietnam to defeat his PTSD.

Amidst a plague-ridden Venice, an overseer starts a progression of exploitative trials to track down a fix.

People find another conscious vegetation somewhere down in the rainforests of Brazil.

The stories of a family that moved to the United States not long before the War of Independence.

Some of the examples of novel writing ideas.

A young lady from India battles to reconnect with her alienated family.

Three outsiders win an escape get-away together

A jumper uncovers government privileged insights covered at the lower part of the sea.

A person goes up against their strange however profoundly genuine anxiety toward being sucked somewhere near the bath channel.

A family goes on a cross-country street outing in the fallout of an atomic conflict.

A gathering of vagrant's endeavour to make their very own home.

A lady is approached a mission to save her sweetheart.

A researcher creates and sells a medication that recoveries lives, however isn't legitimate.

A tale about foreigners during the 1920s and their transition to the United States.

A person endeavors to lay out a congregation gave to the Greek divine beings.

A family battles to persevere through a hotness wave and draft amidst a long summer.

A mother manoeuvres her youngsters toward submitting crimes for her benefit.

A person chooses to bomb every one of their classes to say something.

A town plans for the appointment of its very first Mayer.

A person moves to another town and professes to be somebody they used to be aware.

Two characters go gaga for one another, when they shouldn't.

A person observes a diary with half of the pages filled and attempts to answer their story.

A lady, acting like a minister, is chosen for be the new Pope.

The CEO of an insurance agency manages the means to his very own end exchange.

A robot becomes mindful amidst a conflict it was bought to battle.

A second-hand store proprietor faces the inside clash of selling things they know are significant to other people.

A cop stands up to a misstep they made and stowed away while at work.

A secret society sorts out some way to uncover itself to the remainder of the world.

A person endeavors to uncover the legend of their town.

A person turns back the clock, where they understand they are a higher priority than present day.

A girl embarks to break out her family revile in an unusual manner.

A primitive time story where two significant distance sweethearts' endeavor to interface.

A person endeavors to encounter each sort of affection conceivable.

A researcher uncovers a mysterious entryway that prompts a ground breaking future.

A person is confessed to a profound off the record piece of information that they should safeguard until their passing, regardless of the amount it tortures them.

A dream character kills somebody they despise and should conceal the proof.

A person fosters the ability to change their character, yet have no control over it.

A gathering of characters endeavor to make sense of their encounters going through a desert.

A person hopes to get away from a perilous circumstance in an unfamiliar country.

An authority manages a rising male pioneer undermining her power.

A resigned couple explores life in another country abroad without family.

A person faces their distorted nature and battles to change.

A person lives on the boundary, opposite a general public and culture very different from their own.

A conflict legend gets back and endeavors to make associations with lifelong companions.

How I Make Space for Writing

I'm fortunate in that I can write simply in any place. I travel a lot which implies I invest a great deal of energy in better places with various environmental factors, and by and large, I can make it work in the event that I really want to get something composed.

Despite the fact that I can write in many circumstances, I have learned throughout the long term that I compose considerably more actually when I have a particular encompassing that is generally favourable for my composing efficiency. That is the very thing I attempt to make my composing space at home. Having a quality composing space can help tremendously while I am attempting to compose 2000 words every day.

Regardless of what sort of essayist you will be, you really want a devoted space to work from where you can be imaginative, useful, and work without interruptions.

Whether you have a committed space to change over into your workspace, or you simply have a little corner in your home where you can work, having a motivational work area will do you a ton of good.

Whenever you transform your niche into a composing space planned only for you, your work will feel more like play, and you'll be astounded at the distinction it'll make in your satisfaction and efficiency. A superior composing space will assist you with composing all the more proficiently as everything in that space is there to assist you with being agreeable, getting in the stream, and at last composing better.

It ought to be the sort of room you love working in and the sort of region that moves your most profound inventiveness and concentration.

Effective Mills and Boon's creator expresses that, whenever she had decided to turn into a writer, she transformed one room of her home into a review, locked the entryway, and denied anybody to enter while she was working. You may not feel you need to go very this far however it is essential to save both a space in your home where you can work and make a normal opportunity to compose.

Assuming that you have perused anything on usefulness, and particularly composing efficiency, one of the ideas regularly given is to observe a calm spot in the time you put away to compose. This is basically a valid statement, however, what "calm" signifies will rely a ton upon your very own inclinations. What you truly need to do is observe a space that permits you to compose at an ideal level, and the odds are you will have to explore a decent sum to observe how this precisely affects you.

It would be incredible to make a rundown of the ideal composing space, however in all actuality what works for one author may not work for the following. For instance, I compose much better while having the foundation commotion of music playing, yet I have essayist companions who can't envision having that interruption while attempting to compose. Eventually, you should make your space for you, and that space will probably be not the same as different authors you know. That being said, I can show a portion of the decisions I made while making my space which you can use to think about what might be the best composing space for your requirements.

Track down a decent work area and seat. You need to be agreeable, yet not so agreeable that you lose concentration or nod off. (Your bed's not the best choice for schoolwork, it turns out. You additionally need satisfactory work area to fan out.

Track down a work area or table with a top that rests somewhere close to your midsection and ribcage when you sit at it, so your elbows can rest effectively upon it without slouching your shoulders forward. You likewise need to have the option to rest your feet level on the ground.

Utilize an agreeable seat that fits the tallness of the work area/table. You might need to avoid the fancier work area seats that pivot, roll, lean back, lift, and so on, assuming these will just become interruptions.

Assuming you are utilizing a PC, you maintain that adequate room should put it around 2 to 3 feet from you.

Guarantee sufficient lighting. A review region that is too dull won't just make it more straightforward to fall asleep, it can compound eye strain, which will discourage any review meeting. Cruel lighting, like glaring light, can be awful for your eyes too. Use a work area light to shine light on your work area, and furthermore a close by table or upward light to light up the area.

Assuming that regular light is accessible, absolutely utilize it. Know, however, that while the normal light given by a window can be invigorating and quieting, the compulsion to gaze through the window might hamper your studying. Consider curtains or clear blinds, or face away from the window.

- A restricted area where people can't regularly interrupt
- No TV (I learned early that if there was a TV in the room, it would eventually get turned on and my writing would end)
- Non-commercial music (I write better with background noise, but only with music. I can't listen to the radio where DJs speak as that ruins my writing rhythm)
- No phones (and cell phones turned off)

- A good chair (this is something I didn't realize how important it was until I purchased a good chair)
- A notepad with paper (I like to jot down notes about other possible articles when I write)
- A timer (I set my writing for 20 minutes and then take a break)
- A drink, but no food (A large glass of iced tea is essential, but any food is a distraction.

Those above are a portion of the things I have observed make me more useful when I compose. They could possibly be significant for your composing efficiency. There additionally might just be different things that are significant for you as an essayist which I didn't make reference to. The significant stage to take more time to start to ponder what is significant for you to be in a space which is the most helpful for you to compose at your ideal level, and start making it.

Accumulate your provisions. Ensure you have every one of the materials you want for concentrating on not far off, so you don't sit around idly bumbling around for a ruler or pencil lead tops off.

Keep things coordinated.

Utilize the work area drawers to keep things you really want nearby yet not spread out all around the work area. In the event that you need something more drawers, use boxes, little containers, and so forth that you can stack on the work area along the border of your review region.

Sort out your review materials by course/subject in organizers or folios. Mark each plainly and store them for simple access.

You can likewise sort out tasks and notes by utilizing release sheets, stopper tiles, and divider schedules.

Keep exemplary school supplies like pens or pencils, erasers, paper, notecards, highlighters, etc in allotted regions on the work area or in a convenient cabinet.

Keep a conventional pocket word reference, thesaurus, and number cruncher close by, despite the fact that your telephone can likely do the positions of every one of the three. Utilizing your telephone to do long division or spell-check is an open greeting to interruption in huge numbers different things you can do on it.

Sort out your PC documents, as well. Being coordinated ought to stretch out to your internet-based stuff as well as what's actually around you.

Have you at any point searched for a draft of that paper you were composing just to not be able to track down it?

Or on the other hand lost the notes you expected to read up for your clairvoyant's test since you can't recollect where you saved them?

Make explicit envelopes for each class or subject, and keep every one of your documents in the ideal place. Mark things obviously so you can utilize the pursuit component to track down them. Skip cutesy names for enlightening titles.

Whenever you are writing something that time think about a clock. This relies upon the kind of individual you are. Will a clock propel you to continue to read up for an hour more, or advise you that your number one show is on in just 20 minutes (or make you think I've just been reading up for that long?

Take a stab at utilizing a clock to put forth time-related concentrate on objectives. You can likewise utilize the clock or clock include on your telephone or a watch to assist you with doing this. Choose to study in a "piece" of time, like 40 minutes. Try not to permit yourself any interruptions for that timeframe. At the point when it's up, enjoy some time off to compensate yourself.

You could likewise evaluate a clock for much more exact time-keeping, particularly assuming you are planning for a coordinated test.

If the tick-tock of an antiquated clock irritates you, go advanced.

Reduce desk clutter. This ties in with the need for proper desk organization, but also means that you need to keep tabs on the mess of papers, pens, open books, and so on that may build up on your workspace as you study. Too much clutter can leave you feeling overwhelmed and stressed out, which will put a damper on your study session.

It is a good idea to take short study breaks along the way anyway, so when you do, take a moment to tidy up your workspace before resuming.

Excess clutter can lead to unnecessary distractions. Keep only what you need at that time in front of you. A cluttered workspace can lead to a cluttered mind.

Avoid your phone. It is hard to ignore the lure of your phone when studying. The modern smartphone is perhaps the ultimate tool and the ultimate distractor. Put it away when you study, or you may find yourself browsing Facebook or texting a friend without even realizing you'd picked up the phone.

Turn your phone off or put it in do-not-disturb so the lure of notification chimes doesn't drag you away from your studies. Also try placing it well out of reach so you can't reflexively grab for it.

If you are using your phone as a calculator or other tool, consider putting it on airplane mode which shuts off wireless and cellular connections. You can turn them back on for your (brief) study breaks.

lock out distracting sounds. Some people do well with "white noise," background noises such as those in a coffee shop that aren't really distinct enough to be distracting. Others need total silence to work. Figure out what works well for you, and plan your space accordingly.

"Multitasking" is a myth. You simply can't watch TV or surf Facebook and study at the same time, no matter how much you think you're "really" a multitasker. Focus your study time on studying, and save things like TV and music for leisure time.

If your study space shares a room or a thin wall with a TV in use by someone, or people engaged in conversation or some other potential distraction, try to block out the distraction with your own background noise.

Have a go at picking something like downpour sounds or background noise; are sites and applications with tests of these. In the event that you favour music, attempt light old style or if nothing else something without verses. You need something that discredits sound interruptions without becoming one itself.

Try not to utilize earphones assuming that you have a decision. They appear to frustrate concentration and data maintenance for some individuals, presumably in light of the fact that the sound doesn't as effectively mix out of spotlight.

Utilize the space just for considering. In the event that your review space is your bed, you'll be more enticed to consider (or really) rest. In the event that it's the place where you play PC games, gaming; the lounge area table, eating, etc. You'll be bound to make diverting affiliations.

In the event that it is workable for you to cut out a space - - even a corner, a specialty, an enormous storage room, and so on - - committed solely to examining, get it done. Partner your presence there just with contemplating.

On the off chance that this isn't a choice, give your very best for change the multipurpose space into concentrate on space. Clean up food, dishes, focal points, and so on, from the lounge area table. Set aside your PC games, scrapbooking supplies, etc.

Abstain from nibbling while at the same time composing. composing is difficult, hungry work, yet you should watch out. It's not difficult to snack into insensibility while you're studying. Unhealthy food specifically is an ill-conceived notion. Assuming that you must have a few snacks convenient, pick new organic products, vegetables, or entire grain snacks like saltines.

Attempt to abstain from over-consuming sugar and caffeine while examining. These can cause you to feel nervous and lead to "crashes" later.

Have a go at saving your nibble for when you take a review break. You'll be more mindful of what you're eating, and it's a great method for compensating yourself for a wonderful piece of handiwork.

However, try not to overlook your body's necessities. Set yourself a feast or bite break, or give yourself a particular measure of time before you recharge your espresso. Thusly, you deal with your psyche and your body.

Attempt to find your review space in a space that suits you. On the off chance that you really want dead quiet, observe a concealed corner, a storage room, a storm cellar, an extra room, anything you can find. Assuming that you favor some sound, find it almost an area of greater movement.

In the event that the area can't necessarily in all cases be your devoted review space, let others in on when it is being utilized accordingly.

Feel free to make a

"Don't Disturb,"

"Calm, please,"

"Hello, knock it off, I'm concentrating here!" sign to post, contingent upon your character.

Decorating your review space with banners, signs, and photographs that are critical to you might assist with giving you that lift to continue onward. Simply ensure they don't become interruptions instead of inspirations.

Sort out what sort of inspiration works for you. An image of your family or a cherished pet?

A banner of the vehicle you desire to get after you breeze through these tests and graduate? Duplicates of your prior tests in science with unfortunate scores that not set in stone to enhance? Decide if you want all the more a "push" or a "pull" to keep you spurred.

Brightening the space likewise distinguishes it as yours, regardless of whether just for a brief time, as on account of a lounge area table or shared space. Bring along a couple of rousing tokens for your review time that can be effortlessly gotten together when you're done.

Appeal to your faculties. In the event that you can add tone to your review space, remember that cool tones like blue, purple, and green will generally rouse sensations of harmony and equilibrium, while hotter tones like red, yellow, and orange will more often than not move action and even anxiety.

In this way, in the event that you will generally get excessively restless for forthcoming tests, consider going with a cool shading sense of taste for your stylistic layout; assuming you want a kick in the jeans while attempting to review, go hotter.

However, try not to dupe your different faculties. A few fragrances, similar to lemon, lavender, jasmine, rosemary, cinnamon, and peppermint, appear to support state of mind and efficiency in certain individuals. Evaluate different scented candles and rejuvenating ointments.

While background noise, sounds, or traditional music are by and large the most ideal decisions for foundation sound during a review meeting, in the event that you can't force yourself to pick such choices, select music that is exceptionally natural to you. Make a soundtrack with tunes you've heard multiple times previously; these are bound to blur away from plain sight than another hit that you simply implore you to chime in.

Try not to overdo it. Recollect that the reason for a review space is to assist you with concentrating on more really. On the off chance that you spend an excessively long time attempting to set up your space just so and end up fundamentally decreasing your real review time, you will give yourself a raw deal. A review space intended to restrict interruptions can turn into an interruption itself.

Keep in mind: You're in an ideal situation contemplating in a not-so-great space than not considering in an ideal space.

How do I develop Characters?

You've settled on the idea for your novel. You've narrowed it to a sentence or two, and you're ready to tackle what seems an insurmountable task—developing your lead character.

If you're an Outliner (one who outlines your novel first), it's time for character development, an endeavour not for wimps.

Spellbinding stories feature believable characters who feel knowable.

Yes, even if your genre is Fantasy or Allegory or Futuristic. Your character may even be a superhero, but he must be real and knowable within your premise.

Use male pronouns inclusively here to represent both genders only to avoid the awkward repetition of he/she or him/her, fully recognizing that many lead characters are female and so are most readers.

I'd love to impart some gem that would magically make you an expert at character development. But, sorry, no shortcuts. This is as hard as it sounds. Fail at this task, and it shows.

You cheat your readers when your lead character doesn't develop and grow. No growth, no character arc. No character arc, fewer satisfied readers.

Whether you're writing fiction or genuine, making convincing characters is essential to keeping peruses occupied with your story. There are a huge number to it are trying to make these characters that. How would you bring a person into the story? Which subtleties would it be advisable for you to incorporate about a person? How would you take your characters past the self-evident and tasteless?

The greatest mix-up new essayists make is presenting their principle character past the point of no return. Generally speaking, he ought to be the principal individual in front of an audience and the peruser ought to have the option to connect his name with how they see him.

Naming your personality can be nearly basically as unpleasant as naming an infant. You need something fascinating and vital, yet not eccentric or absurd. Pass on Blaze Starr and Goodnight Robichaud to the dramas. (In reality, I wish I'd considered Goodnight Robichaud; Ethan Hawke plays him in The Magnificent Seven.)

Purposeful anecdotes call for telling names like Prudence and Truth and Pride, yet present day ones ought to be more inconspicuous. I composed a Christmas anecdote where the principle character was Tom Douten (get it? Questioning Thomas), and his fiancee was Noella (Christmasy, an adherent to Santa) Wright (Miss Right).

For standard books, normal names are forgettable. Identity is significant. You shouldn't have a Greek named Bubba Jackson.

You want to associate peruser and character, so the name ought to mirror his legacy and maybe even indicate his character. In The Green Mile, Stephen King named a frail, apprehensive person Percy Wetmore. Normally, we treat legends with more regard.

Give naming the time it needs. Search online for child names of the two genders, and most records will sort these by nationality.

Be certain the name is all things considered and topographically exact. You wouldn't have characters named Jaxon and Brandi, for example, in a story set in Elizabethan England.

I frequently allude to World Almanacs to track down names for unfamiliar characters. I'll match the principal name of a present government pioneer in that country with the last name of one of their authentic figures (however not one so renowned that the peruser contemplates whether he's connected, as François Bonaparte).

You need a reasonable image of your personality in your inner consciousness, yet don't wrongly drive your peruser to see him precisely the manner in which you do. Without a doubt, tallness, hair and eye tone, and genuineness (athletic or not) are significant.

Be that as it may, does it truly matter whether your peruser envisions your blonde champion as Gwyneth Paltrow or Charlize Theron? Or on the other hand your dull haired legend as George Clooney or Ben Affleck?

As I instruct with respect to portrayals of the sky and the climate and settings, it's critical that your depiction of your fundamental person isn't delivered as a different component. Rather, layer in what he resembles through exchange and during the activity.

Indicate barely to the point of setting off the theatre of the peruser's psyche so he frames his own psychological picture.

Great many pursuers could have large number of somewhat differed pictures of the person, which is OK, gave you've given him enough data to know whether your legend is huge or little, alluring or not, and athletic or not.

Whether you're an Outliner (generally meeting your personality as though he were sitting directly before you) or a Pantser (getting to know him as he uncovers himself to you), the more you are familiar him, the better you will recount your story.

How old would he say he is?

What is his identity?

Does he have scars? Piercings? Tattoos? Actual flaws? Distortions?

What does his voice seem like?

Does he have a complement?

Perusers regularly have trouble separating one person from another, so in the event that you can give him a tag, as an extraordinary signal or peculiarity, that helps put him aside.

Origin story is all that is occurred before Chapter 1.

- Dig profound.

- What has molded your personality into the individual he is today?
- Things you ought to be aware, regardless of whether you remember them for your book:
- Whenever, where, and to whom he was conceived
- Family, their names and ages
- Where he went to secondary school, school, and graduate school
- Political association
- Occupation
- Pay
- Objectives
- Abilities and gifts
- Profound life
- Companions
- Dearest companion
- Whether he's single, dating, or wedded
- Perspective
- Character type
- Outrage triggers
- Delights, joys
- Dread

Furthermore, whatever else pertinent involved

Character Development Step 4. Ensure he's human, powerless, and defective

Indeed, even superheroes have imperfections and shortcomings. For Superman, there's Kryptonite. For swashbucklers like Indiana Jones, there are snakes.

A lead character without human characteristics is difficult to relate to. Yet, ensure his blemishes aren't huge issues. They ought to be trivial, reasonable, recognizable.

Be mindful so as not to make your legend irredeemable - for example, a weakling, a lily liver, a good-for-nothing, a moron, or a goof ball (like a cop who fails to remember his weapon or his ammo).

You need a person with whom your peruser can relate, and to do that, he should be powerless.

Make occasions that quietly display strength of character and soul. For instance, does your personality recognize a server and perceive her by name? Could he treat a clerk the same way he treats his agent?

Assuming that he's behind schedule, yet witnesses a crisis, does he pause and help?

These are called pet-the-canine minutes, where a generally greater than-life character accomplishes something unusual something that may be considered underneath him.

Perusers recollect such powerful episodes, and they make your personality's advancement much more emotional.

It was George Bailey's forfeiting his movement the-world dreams to assume control over the humble reserve funds and credit that made his confronting the disgusting Mr. Potter so brave in the exemplary film It's a Wonderful Life.

Need to transform your Jimmy Stewart into a George Bailey?

Make him genuine.

Give him a pet-the-canine second.

While endeavouring to make your primary person genuine and human, make certain to likewise make him brave or embed inside him basically the possibility to be chivalrous.

Eventually, after he has advanced every one of the illustrations, he really wants to from his disappointments to escape the awful difficulty you dove him into, he should adapt to the situation and score an extraordinary moral triumph.

He can have a soft spot for chocolates or an anxiety toward snakes, yet he should appear and acknowledge the cold hard truth when the opportunity arrives.

An all-around created character ought to be exceptional, yet interesting. Never permit your hero to be the person in question. It is surely alright to permit him to confront obstructions and difficulties, yet never depict him as a weakling or a defeatist.

Give your personality characteristics that charm and propel the peruser to proceed. For instance:

a person with an unassuming childhood (a longshot) adapts to the situation

a person with a secret strength or capacity unobtrusively uncovers it right off the bat in the story and later purposes it in an uncommon or phenomenal manner

Make him brave, and you'll make him remarkable.

What actually occurs in the novel is a certain something. Your legend needs inconvenience, an issue, a journey, a test, something that drives the story.

Yet, similarly as significant is your personality's essential inner turmoil. This will decide his internal discourse. Developing inside will for the most part offer more to your Character Arc than the surface story.

Ask yourself:

What keeps him alert around evening time?

What is his vulnerable side?

What are his mysteries?

What humiliates him?

What energy drives him?

Blend and match subtleties from individuals you know - and yourself - to make both the internal and external individual. Whenever he faces what is happening, you'll know how he ought to answer.

The fun of being an author is getting to encapsulate the characters we expound on. I can be a little youngster, an elderly person, a kid, a dad, a grandma, another race, a scalawag, of an alternate political or profound influence, and so forth. The rundown continues and the conceivable outcomes are huge.

The most effective way to foster a person is to, basically, become that person.

Envision yourself experiencing the same thing he finds himself, confronting each difficulty, responding to each address how might you respond on the off chance that you were your personality?

Assuming your personality ends up in human peril, envision yourself in that dilemma. Perhaps you've never experienced something like this, however you can summon it in your psyche. Recollect the last time you felt in harm's way, increase that by a thousand, and become your personality.

What went through your head when you accepted you were home alone and heard strides across the floor above?

I'll be straightforward, there is an undeniable issue in writing with regards to variety.

You can discuss this all you need, yet coming from somebody who peruses many books, it's an undeniable issue that main you and different journalists going ahead can address.

Your book ought to be similarly essentially as different as this present reality.

If you don't have characters with differing skin, hair, or eye tones alongside changing body types, incapacities, and, surprisingly, psychological sicknesses, your characters are not adequately different.

You don't need to compose a book about these things for you to remember them for your book.

For instance, one of my principle characters have elevated degrees of uneasiness. His storyline doesn't rotate around this dysfunctional behaviour; however, it is there, seen, and can influence his plot.

Oppose the compulsion to expound on something you haven't encountered prior to directing careful examination.

Creative mind can take you just up until this point. However, you can risk everything and the kitchen sink time you surmise about something, clever perusers will call you on it. For example, I can envision myself as a lady. I had a mother, I have a spouse, I have girls in-regulation and granddaughters, a female associate, ladies' partners.

So, I can speculate about their sentiments and feelings, however I'll generally be disabled by the basic reality that I'm not a lady. I as of late ran into a close buddy who let me know she was destitute.

I referenced to certain ladies' companions that I questioned her since she looked set up, as though she'd been to the magnificence shop.

I said, "Assuming you were living in your vehicle, could you burn through cash on finishing your hair and nails?"

Normally that is the last thing a man would contemplate. In any case, ladies in my circle said, sure, they could see it. Disguising your quandary and keeping a bit of dignity would merit avoiding a couple of dinners.

Let's assume you're expounding on what you'd feel on the off chance that you lost a kid. I truly want to believe that you would just be speculating about such a ghastliness, however to expound on it with believability takes intensive examination.

You'd need to meet with somebody who has persevered through such a misfortune and had the opportunity to have the option to discuss it.

Is your personality an instructor? A cop? A CEO? Or on the other hand the individual from one more calling with which you have no private experience?

Invest energy in a homeroom, interview an instructor, organize a ride-alongside a cop, interview a CEO. Try not to put together your legend with respect to pictures from films and TV shows.

The last thing you need is a generalization perusers can't relate to and whom some would see through immediately.

You'll observe that the vast majority love discussing their lives and callings.

How to be the disciplined Writer

"I compose when I'm enlivened, and I make sure that I'm roused at ten o'clock each day"

Assuming you are considering turning into a writer, you must foster your discipline as a writer however much as could be expected.

Recall that composing extraordinary substance takes a lot of work, and assuming you need discipline, you'll struggle with finishing what has been started.

Nonetheless, it very well may be a piece challenging to foster your composing discipline.

So, you will require a set arrangement on the best way to upgrade it.

At some point or another, most writers find that the most troublesome aspect of composing isn't devising characters or consummating our sentences or learning story structure. No, the hardest piece of finishing some composing is simply making it happen. Stopping is a hotly debated issue among writers for the very explanation that practically we all battle to keep up with the sheer power of will regularly expected in just putting our fingers to the console and making them move.

Energy might have incited an interest in this methodology, however what we're referring to is discipline, straightforward as can be. But as significant as discipline might be in keeping us at the work area, it isn't sufficient. Whenever life gets genuine, discipline might carry us to the work area, yet it can't necessarily in every case make the words stream.

How to start and maintain writing even when it's hard is an evergreen subject among writers. In any case, it's especially appropriate at the present time, partially because more individuals than any time in recent memory are investigating those accounts, they've for a long time needed to tell.

This is an extraordinary opportunity to investigate our energy for composing, both on the grounds that excitement can be more diligently to access during stress and furthermore because energy is an intensely sure feeling that can bring a lot of good into your life.

I used to say discipline in writing came down to "determination, maturity, determination." And it does to an extent. But determination is a restricted source. If you don't help it with great behaviours, it will ultimately run out.

If you're reliable in disciplining yourself to show up at the desk for at minimum a month, your habitual brain will take over and you'll find you need to use less and less determination.

There will silent be days when those habits are dared by outside conditions but showing up at your desk for the 30th day in a row (or, even better, the $7,000^{th}$ which is approximately where I'm at after 16+ years of regular writing) is a whole lot easier than showing up sporadically for 30 days spread out over a longer period.

Discipline is directly linked to enthusiasm. If your motivation for sitting down to write is strong, then the discipline will follow.

By the same token, if you're struggling with discipline, check your motivation.

How bad do you really want to write this story?

To be a writer?

To have a daily writing practice?

"I also do fifteen minutes of meditation right before starting my morning fiction writing. I found that helps me focus"

At the point when you are prepared to write, you might end up with your fingers floating over the console, drifting, drifting, floating.

In no time, twenty minutes have passed.

I've observed that setting a brief time frame limit, like twenty minutes, and afterward making a plunge and composing like insane will get me moving and move me along.

Composing for twenty minutes doesn't appear as scary as composing for a little while.

Whenever the twenty minutes is up, I start one round.

The problem is, really, that people SAY that if you sit in that chair in front of your computer long enough and WRITE, that the Muse will obediently appear.

The truth is, as far as I have experienced, writing is partially a matter of willing the muse to come and pull up a chair next to you, sip tea and chat while you wildly type all the brilliant ideas about all the great characters and conflicts.

The trick, I believe is, to set up a place that is quite comfortable for the Muse and to invite him very cordially and wait very patiently for that presence and then don't EVER rush him out the door before the visit is over.

Probably the most effective way you could foster your discipline, is to follow a set composing plan.

If you have any desire to refine your composing style, practice is critical.

Be that as it may, there will be times where you won't want to compose.

There will be times where you don't feel inventive.

On the off chance that you don't have a set composing plan, you will doubtlessly leave the composition for some other time.

When follow a composing plan, you will want to make composing a propensity.

Besides having a set composing plan, one way you could guarantee that you get the greater part of your composing meetings, is to have a set word count. The word count relies upon you. It very well may associate with 2000 words each day assuming you are an amateur, or it very well may be 4000 if you are more capable. Everything truly relies upon you. What is important is that you could keep satisfying the word consider reliably as could be expected.

Or in another way, assuming you send off into writing a book endeavouring to compose numerous parts in each writing meeting, missing the mark simple. Discipline outgrows making little strides more than once. Compose 100 words today, then, at that point, 200 tomorrow. Partition scenes into portions marked 'a', 'b', 'c, etc, and resolve to simply handle section 'a' today, and b tomorrow.

To start writing or building a story or characters, you need to connect yourself with your childhood memories or some incidences.

All my most clear cherished recollections happen outside-going around my life as a youngster area, building mud posts, digging burrows, riding ponies, climbing trees.

In addition to the fact that nature is a strong wellspring of mending and motivation, for large numbers of us it is likewise an immediate line to our freewheeling youth excitement.

To the extent that you're capable, inundate yourself in nature.

Indeed, even filling your home with plants and real time nature recordings on your TV can be strong.

Besides making new satisfied consistently, it is likewise smart to peruse new happy consistently.

By perusing new happy consistently, you will want to renew your store of composing thoughts.

Perusing new satisfied will likewise permit you to contrast your composing style with different essayists.

This isn't intended to cause you to really regret your composing abilities.

It is intended to provoke you to compose better happy.

The creative cycle could be a to some degree desolate experience since you will do the greater part of the writing without anyone else. In any case, it shouldn't be a desolate undertaking. You could join a writing group. The writing could be in your area or on the web. It doesn't exactly make any difference what sort of writing group you join.

What makes a difference is that you have a care group that will assist you with developing as a writer.

Besides making new happy consistently, it is additionally smart to peruse new satisfied consistently.

By perusing new satisfied consistently, you will want to renew your store of composing thoughts.

Perusing new happy will likewise permit you to contrast your composing style with different journalists.

This isn't intended to cause you to regret your composing abilities.

It is intended to provoke you to compose better satisfied.

Enthusiasm is a flow of joy. But if other, less pleasant emotions are dammed up, eventually joy won't flow either.

If you feel disconnected from your enthusiasm, consider whether you're disconnected from other emotions as well.

If you carry a lot of tension in your body, this is often a sign of bottled-up emotions.

Particularly in an emotional and anxious time, there is tremendous value in working through backed-up emotions.

Once the tears finish flowing, joy will flow again too. There are many resources available for this (including Cameron's morning pages), but one of the most helpful to me has been yoga.

Getting "into my body" and feeling my emotions physically was and is key.

To upgrade your discipline, it is smart to take up reflection. One of the most pervasive issues you could look during the creative cycle, is an absence of concentration.

This absence of concentrate normally originates from a powerlessness to calm one's contemplations and nerves.

This is the place where contemplation proves to be useful.

By taking up contemplation, you will want to calm your inward considerations, and be completely at the time.

I hope that all my own experienced suggestions will help you to became as a discipline writer.

How do I Improve Vocabulary

I born and brought up in Marathi family. I am originally Marathi. My mother tongue is Marathi. When I started to learn English that time i was thrilled by experiencing my own reactions.
the first reactions were towards my Marathi thinking and second was my translator. Whenever I use to talk in English before that I use to prepare sentence or words in Marathi in my brain and then i use to translate it in English. it ate too much time of mine.
Further many things came into picture about English language such as pronunciation, words, sentence,

grammar and importantly vocabulary. i worked on each aspect of it.

Learned.

Practiced for many times.

Read many books etc.

Therefore, now a days I am speaking, writing, and importantly thinking in English.

"Thinking in English" will improve your novel writing skills. you can build up story with the help of different characters with different aspects.

you can easily imagine that "what characters are saying"

"What they want to do"

"What they feel"

"What they want to eat"?

"What are the hobbies of the characters"

"What are the positive and negative points of the characters"

"What are the Characters enemies in their own life"

this all information you can think and write about your story characters and bold up the story.

To build up a story characters or story, thinking is important and for thinking vocabulary is important. therefore, here I would like to explain some of the good ideas that I used during writing on "how to increase vocabulary"

These ideas will defiantly help you to increase your vocabulary.

It's obviously true that if we have any desire to communicate in a language fluidly, we just need to know a normal of 2,500 detached and 2,000 dynamic word-families to deal with most sorts of our discussions. That is 4.5% of the accessible 100,000-word families in English. English locals know around 10,000 to 20,000 words. Yet something out there, isn't that so?

Before you begin filling the holes, I propose to make your task an energy or to absolutely become energetic about finding intriguing, particular, or seldom utilized words. Welcome obscure words, have a go at speculating their importance, contemplate their purposes. It very well may be a stunner!

If you have any desire to be coordinated, here we go:

What is the fundamental objective and reason? Is it for work, tests, or individual reasons?

What number of new words? What is your period and timetable? Each day, week, year.

In which explicit regions you might want to develop?

Plan your exercises. Stick to 15 minutes per day.

Prepare your stuff, for example word reference, thesaurus, streak cards, worksheets.

Research shows that by far most of words are gained from setting. It may not be underscored enough, as learning in setting of circumstances and sentences has immense advantages for every one of the three parts of jargon securing learning, review, and maintenance.

Jargon ought to continuously be learnt in setting not in segregation.

There are numerous approaches to bringing setting into the jargon learning, the most straightforward being to learn jargon in sentences. This has extra advantages of acquainting the peruses with a few words all at once and explaining their significance which may not generally be clear from a basic word reference interpretation.

Past sentences, one can explore different avenues regarding learning words with stories, melodies, or simply regular circumstances.

For example, as opposed to learning weather conditions related words all alone, investigate a weather conditions figure on the web, and attempt to envision a discussion about climate one week from now, and what it will mean for the cookout one has been anticipating to such an extent.

All things considered utilizing jargon can assist it with staying to you. Compose sentences with new jargon words or create a story utilizing a gathering of words or articulations. Assuming that you are making the rounds, you can make the model sentences to you on the off chance that you don't have a pen and paper helpful.

Words are like pictures. The more we see them the more straightforward we perceive and get to know them. Ravenous perusing can be one strong key, especially to improve your composition.

It's certain that perusing is the best method for getting new jargon. At the point when you read, you see words being utilized in setting - and that makes it significantly more compelling than, for instance, just remembering word records.

With setting data encompassing each new word, there's a decent opportunity you can figure its significance just by getting the general text. Figuring out the significance of words in such a manner is the normal approach to learning language-and perusing gives the best an open door to get presented to this regular approach to learning.

If you're not ready to construe the significance of new words while perusing, it's presumably because there are an excessive number of obscure words in the text. All things considered, take a stab at perusing simpler materials. The way to great perusing is making it a pleasurable movement. Try not to fear going over obscure words, yet ensure the text is proper for your understanding level.

Nonetheless, despite everything that a few sites and jargon educators might say to you, perusing isn't the most important thing in the world of further developing your assertion pool. There is no sense in perusing a 500-page book if you are simply going to get 1/3 of the text! Perusing is anyway a gigantically significant part to fabricate and further develop jargon firmly. These elements are essential to successfully move toward material:

Unless you apply speed perusing procedures it's smarter to require some investment and simply partake in the understanding system. You might need to move toward your message on a word-by-word, sentence by sentence premise. This is likewise where the word reference and thesaurus prove to be useful. Get that word reference and turn the word upward and how to articulate it!

Depending on your age or perusing and information level hold back nothing is made for you but at the same time is trying in a positive manner. Sci-fi and dream books are an extraordinary wellspring of non-existent words, while genuine material will build your jargon on a more scholastic level. Understanding books or books about contemporary points will help get to learn jargon that is new and wasn't around a couple of years prior.

As engaging as the most recent big name tattle magazine might be, without help from anyone else, it won't show you the wide assortment of words you will be hoping to learn. Frequently the most valuable perusing material accessible for building your jargon are exemplary books from writing greats. While they might take more time to process and comprehend, this perusing source will likewise show you exactly the way that specific words can be used in discussion and depiction.

The incredible thing about book recordings is that you can find them pretty much anyplace, from online sources to your neighbourhood library. Plug in your earphones and do just tune in! Regardless of whether you comprehend each word you hear; it will show you the specific elocution and situation of each word. What's more if you really do get each word? Then that is shockingly better. Words are regularly made much clearer when set into setting and utilized in discussion, and as an audience, you will likewise be given an intriguing and connecting with story for sure. Open Culture and Loyal Books are two incredible spots to begin.

Each and all of us carries on without an alternate life every day, and yours could well be one of the additional fascinating ones out there.

Why not expound on it?

This will have 2 principle benefits. It will urge you to record words consistently, and the more agreeable you become with composing and utilizing said words, the almost certain you are to involve them later. Observe that your composing is utilizing similar words over and over? Utilize your thesaurus to view as a decent other option. This will, thus, give you one more word to use in your ordinary composition and discussion!

Whilst you won't be supposed to compose the following hit single for Beyoncé or Iggy Azalea, recording a tune or sonnet with a basic, yet clear rhyming example can be an incredible device to utilize while attempting to recall new words. What about composing a sonnet that contains a specific word and what it implies? Assuming it rhymes with another word that you are attempting to realize, that is far better. If you have any desire to take the verse course, then, at that point, Poem of Quotes is an enormously charming, simple to follow site.

Human creatures love records. They make exercises clear to comprehend, they maintain everything under control, and you can likewise effectively monitor your advancement in an assortment of exercises.

Henceforth, why not use them while attempting to grow your jargon?

Decide of comparable words utilizing your thesaurus, suppose fifteen expressions of a comparable significance each rundown. You should simply go through 10-15 minutes every day retaining this rundown, ensuring you can recall every single word on there. Choices are proficient projects that accompany a form in work sheet maker.

Find that the rundown isn't working for you? Attempt mind-planning all things considered. Mind maps make the associations between specific subjects staggeringly clear, and whenever utilized accurately can be a significant resource while growing your jargon. They will likewise permit you to give instances of words being used, something you are restricted with if you decide to develop records.

Connect

It's more straightforward to remember words considering a typical subject. Make your own associations among words and potentially sort out them in a bug graph or on similar pages of your note pad. The topic may be a theme or circumstance (E.g., words for discussing nature), phrasal action words utilizing a typical word or words that share a language point practically speaking.

Befriend the Dictionary

A word reference is the principal irreplaceable asset to work on your jargon. It's exclusively by looking into a word in a word reference that you will become familiar with its exact significance, spelling, substitute definitions, and track down extra helpful data about it. A thesaurus is likewise a significant asset for learning by tracking down associations between words, like their equivalents and antonyms.

Consider adding a decent word reference and thesaurus to your shelf.

A word can have various implications and shades of significance, the creator or speaker might have involved the word in an alternate setting and regardless of whether one speculation the right importance, there are chances of confusing. Keep the definitions short, set it to your own tone and promptly record it in your jargon journal. One can't comprehend and recollect the word on the off chance that one can't make sense of it oneself.

Additionally, write down the way to express the word phonetically in a manner you can comprehend. For instance, for "sideways," elocution could be composed as "gracious bleak." Try the e-word references which have a button to snap to hear the articulation.

As well as involving the proper word in the applicable spot, elocution is similarly significant. Articulating the words erroneously is more terrible than not utilizing the words by any stretch of the imagination. In the wake of recording the legitimate elocution, the word should be said resoundingly a few times.

Really look at the thesaurus and record the word's equivalents and antonyms to comprehend what the word meant better and assuming the circumstance requests, even draw an image that can assist you with recollecting its significance.

Act

Get you continues by carrying on words and articulations you learn. Or then again, envision and showcase a circumstance where you would have to utilize them. Assuming you have a showcase a word or articulation from your note pad and check whether the individual in question can think about what it then, at that point, trade over and attempt to think about the thing your accomplice is carrying on. If you are distant from everyone else, utilize a mirror and imagine you are having a discussion with somebody utilizing your new jargon.

Play words games

The extraordinary thing about the web is that games are in a real sense all over and there are many to altogether work on your jargon. Close by customary top choices, for example, word-look, you can observe shooters, vehicle driving games and flip cards, all of which will introduce new words to you in a pleasant, inviting climate. Many websites are there that takes special care of a wide assortment of understudies, from kids to grown-ups and furthermore has a gigantically pleasant choice of games.

If a customary or versatile web association is an issue, sit back and relax! Itemized in area 7 is exactly the way in which you can make word arrangements of comparable words that will assist you with your remembering of these words. Make a word-search or a crossword on your Microsoft word, or just build one with a pen and paper. Include the rundown of words you need to learn for the afternoon, and off you go.

We all have a cabinet or a little pantry where we put the family pre-packaged games. Top picks, for example, Scrabble and Boggle can all go a workable approach to working on your words, and, assuming you have a word reference nearby, you can learn and have a good time while setting out your letters. On the off chance that you have no games in your pantry. An excursion down to your nearby vehicle boot deal or to Amazon Retailers will give you one.

The utilization of blaze cards is quite possibly the best method for learning new data. Add words in with the general mishmash, and you will see your pace of memory maintenance shoot upwards. Think of some interesting, or difficult to learn words onto your cards and afterward have a go with them, and watch your remembrance shoot upwards.

Utilize new words in regular language!

Chat with individuals: Nothing out there beats really engrossing yourself in a climate where you are urged to involve those words however much as could be expected. For this specific road of investigation, this implies conversing with however many individuals as could be expected under the circumstances. Take part in ordinary discussion, regardless of how essential and take a stab at utilizing a couple of your learnt words while conversing with someone. Perceive how they respond, check whether you get reaction. If not? Then attempt once more. It is all important for the learning system, achievement or not! Lite Mind has a few extraordinary ideas on this subject, as well as a couple of different thoughts you might wish to attempt. [Editor's note: The Couch is likewise an incredible spot to do this in Melbourne - and they have free food!]

Are you on a web-based discussion zeroed in on your style advantages? Your #1 football crew? Your #1 leisure activity? Utilize this for your potential benefit! The incredible thing about imparting through an internet-based medium is that it is less quick in nature than an up close and personal discussion, so you can plan and consider cautiously about your reaction.

Broaden

Accomplish something else from your everyday daily practice: hunting, fishing, or writing for a blog any movement that isn't a piece of your ordinary life can turn into an incredible method for learning new words, as each specialty has its own language and extraordinary approaches to conveying. Peruse various books and magazines than the ones you're utilized to. Watch unknown dialect films. Take up new leisure activities, spend time with various individuals.

Study Session
1. Prepare your daily routine

----

2. Enlist your daily Chores

----

3. Design the rough time layout for daily chores

----

4. Manage the work and daily chores time

----

5. Find out waste time in whole day.

----

6. Find out your passionate topic of interest for writing

----

7. Start researching, reviewing, & draft writing

----

8. Prepare drafts

----

9. Correct drafts and send manuscript for publishing

----

10. Enjoy the Book writing, proof reading and publishing process.

About the Author

Rohit Shankar Mane

Dr. Rohit Shankar Mane is Microbiology Scientist. His educational qualification is B.Sc. M.Sc. NET. DPM. PGDFSQM. Ph.D., He is Principal Investigator of DST, DBT and National geography research projects. He is inventor of ROVE sterilization method. He is fellow of Dr. Babasaheb Ambedkar National Research Fellowship, BARTI, India. He has given International Young scientist award by AEI, India. He has given National Young Scientist award by American Microbiology Society of America. He is the 4th runner up of Citrinin against MCF-7 cell line at Dr. Raghunath Mashelkar Award, India. His project entitled "Chitinase and their antifungal effects" got nominated for GYTI-2018 award under Indian government. He has published 32 Books and 56 research papers at International and National level. He is reviewer of 26 International Journals and associate editor of 12 International Journals. His interested research area is Microbiology and Agriculture. He is member of American Microbiology Society of America and Canadian Microbiology Society of Canada. He is founder and Director of "Scientist R academy" Research and Publication Institute of India. He is poet, activist and always engaged in microbiology awareness programs.

www.ingramcontent.com/pod-product-compliance
Lightning Source LLC
LaVergne TN
LVHW041853070526
838199LV00045BB/1587